MR. NOISY

by Roger Hargreaves

Mr Noisy was a very, very noisy person indeed.

For example.

If Mr Noisy was reading this story to you, he'd be shouting at the top of his voice.

And the top of Mr Noisy's voice is a very loud place indeed.

You can hear it a hundred miles away!

MR NOISY

For example.

When most people sneeze you can hear them in the next room.

But . . . ATISHOO.

When Mr Noisy sneezes you can hear him in the next country!

Now, this story starts when Mr Noisy was asleep in bed, in his bedroom, in his house, which is on top of a hill.

He was snoring.

And, as you can well imagine, when Mr Noisy snores, that is a snore worth hearing.

It sounds more like a herd of elephants than a snore!

Then Mr Noisy's alarm clock went off.

Mr Noisy's alarm clock sounds like no other alarm clock in the world.

It sounds more like a fire engine!

Mr Noisy woke up.

And so too did all the people who lived in Wobbletown, which is at the bottom of Mr Noisy's hill.

Later that day, Mr Noisy decided that he had to go shopping.

He went out of his house, shutting the door behind him.

BANG!

The door wobbled. The house wobbled. The whole hill wobbled.

Wobbletown wobbled. Even a bird, flying high above, wobbled!

Then Mr Noisy walked down the hill.

CLUMP! CLUMP! CLUMP!

He walked into the baker's shop.

CRASH went the door as he opened it.

BANG went the door as he shut it.

"I'D LIKE A LOAF OF BREAD," boomed Mr Noisy to Mrs Crumb, the baker's wife.

Mrs Crumb trembled, and sold him a loaf.

Then Mr Noisy walked along the street to the butcher.

CLUMP! CLUMP! CLUMP!

He walked into the butcher's shop.

CRASH went the door as he opened it.

BANG went the door as he shut it.

"I'D LIKE A PIECE OF MEAT," boomed Mr Noisy to Mr Bacon, the butcher.

Mr Bacon trembled, and sold him some meat.

Afterwards, Mrs Crumb met Mr Bacon in the street.

"We really must do something about Mr Noisy being so noisy," she said.

"Absolutely," replied Mr Bacon. "But what?"

"I know," said Mrs Crumb, and she whispered into Mr Bacon's ear.

Mr Bacon smiled a small smile, which grew into a broad grin.

"Mrs Crumb," he said, "I think you have the answer!"

The following day Mr Noisy again went shopping down to Wobbletown.

CLUMP! CLUMP! CLUMP!

He went into Mrs Crumb's shop.

"I'D LIKE A LOAF OF BREAD," he boomed.

"Sorry! What did you say?" asked Mrs Crumb, pretending not to hear.

"I'D LIKE A LOAF OF BREAD!!" Mr Noisy shouted.

"Sorry," said Mrs Crumb, putting her hand to her ear. "Can you speak up please!"

"I'D . . . LIKE . . . A . . . LOAF . . . OF . . . BREAD!!!" roared Mr Noisy.

"Can't hear you," replied Mrs Crumb.

Mr Noisy gave up, and went out.

Mr Noisy went into Mr Bacon's shop.

"I'D LIKE A PIECE OF MEAT," he boomed.

Mr Bacon pretended not to notice.

"I'D LIKE A PIECE OF MEAT!!" Mr Noisy shouted.

"Did you say something?" asked Mr Bacon.

"I . . . SAID . . . I'D . . . LIKE . . . A . . . PIECE . . . OF . . . MEAT!!!" roared Mr Noisy.

"Pardon?" said Mr Bacon.

Mr Noisy gave up.

And went out.

And went home.

And went to bed.

Hungry!

The day after Mr Noisy tried again.

He went into Mrs Crumb's shop.

"I'D LIKE A LOAF OF BREAD," he boomed.

"A what?" asked Mrs Crumb.

Mr Noisy started shouting at the very top of his voice.

"A . . . LOAF . . . OF . . ." and then he stopped. And then he thought.

And then he said, quietly, "I'd like a loaf of bread, please, Mrs Crumb."

Mrs Crumb smiled.

"Certainly," she said.

Then Mr Noisy went into Mr Bacon's shop.

"I'D LIKE A PIECE OF MEAT," he boomed.

"Did you say something?" asked Mr Bacon.

"YES . . . I . . . DID," shouted Mr Noisy at the very, very top of his voice.

"I . . . SAID . . . I'D . . . LIKE . . . A . . ." and then he stopped. And then he thought.

And then he said, quietly, "I'd like a piece of meat, please, Mr Bacon."

Mr Bacon smiled.

"My pleasure," he said.

So, carrying his bread and his meat, Mr Noisy set off home, up the hill.

CLUMP! CLUMP! CLUMP!

Then he stopped. Then he thought. And then, do you know what he did?

He tiptoed!

A tiptoe was something Mr Noisy had never tried before.

It was fun!

Mr Noisy arrived at his front door.

He put out his hand to open the door, and then he stopped. And then he thought. And then, do you know what he did?

He opened the door – very quietly.

He stepped inside.

And then he shut the door – very gently.

Quietly and gently were two things Mr Noisy had never tried before either.

That was fun too!

And do you know something?

From then until now, Mr Noisy isn't anything like as noisy as he used to be.

And do you know something else?

The people of Wobbletown are delighted – especially Mrs Crumb and Mr Bacon.

And do you know something else?

Mr Noisy has learned how to whisper!

3 Great Offers for MR.MEN Fans!

MR.MEN TOKEN

CUT ALONG DOTTED LINE AND RETURN THIS WHOLE PAGE

1 New Mr. Men or Little Miss Library Bus Presentation Cases

A brand new stronger, roomier school bus library box, with sturdy carrying handle and stay-closed fasteners.
The full colour, wipe-clean boxes make a great home for your full collection.
They're just £5.99 inc P&P and free bookmark!

☐ MR. MEN ☐ LITTLE MISS (please tick and order overleaf)

2 Door Hangers and Posters

In every Mr. Men and Little Miss book like this one, you will find a special token. Collect 6 tokens and we will send you a brilliant Mr. Men or Little Miss poster and a Mr. Men or Little Miss double sided full colour bedroom door hanger of your choice. Simply tick your choice in the list and tape a 50p coin for your two items to this page.

Door Hangers (please tick)

- ☐ Mr. Nosey & Mr. Muddle
- ☐ Mr. Slow & Mr. Busy
- ☐ Mr. Messy & Mr. Quiet
- ☐ Mr. Perfect & Mr. Forgetful
- ☐ Little Miss Fun & Little Miss Late
- ☐ Little Miss Helpful & Little Miss Tidy
- ☐ Little Miss Busy & Little Miss Brainy
- ☐ Little Miss Star & Little Miss Fun

Posters (please tick)

- ☐ MR.MEN
- ☐ LITTLE MISS

PLEASE STICK YOUR 50P COIN HERE

3 Sixteen Beautiful Fridge Magnets – any 2 for £2.00! inc.P&P

They're very special collector's items!
Simply tick your first and second* choices from the list below of any 2 characters!

1st Choice

☐ Mr. Happy
☐ Mr. Lazy
☐ Mr. Topsy-Turvy
☐ Mr. Bounce
☐ Mr. Bump
☐ Mr. Small
☐ Mr. Snow
☐ Mr. Wrong
☐ Mr. Daydream
☐ Mr. Tickle
☐ Mr. Greedy
☐ Mr. Funny
☐ Little Miss Giggles
☐ Little Miss Splendid
☐ Little Miss Naughty
☐ Little Miss Sunshine

2nd Choice

☐ Mr. Happy
☐ Mr. Lazy
☐ Mr. Topsy-Turvy
☐ Mr. Bounce
☐ Mr. Bump
☐ Mr. Small
☐ Mr. Snow
☐ Mr. Wrong
☐ Mr. Daydream
☐ Mr. Tickle
☐ Mr. Greedy
☐ Mr. Funny
☐ Little Miss Giggles
☐ Little Miss Splendid
☐ Little Miss Naughty
☐ Little Miss Sunshine

*Only in case your first choice is out of stock.

TO BE COMPLETED BY AN ADULT

To apply for any of these great offers, ask an adult to complete the coupon below and send it with the appropriate payment and tokens, if needed, to MR. MEN CLASSIC OFFER, PO BOX 715, HORSHAM RH12 5WG

☐ Please send ____ Mr. Men Library case(s) and/or ____ Little Miss Library case(s) at £5.99 each inc P&P
☐ Please send a poster and door hanger as selected overleaf. I enclose six tokens plus a 50p coin for P&P
☐ Please send me ____ pair(s) of Mr. Men/Little Miss fridge magnets, as selected above at £2.00 inc P&P

Fan's Name ______________________________

Address ______________________________

______________________________ **Postcode** ____________

Date of Birth ______________________________

Name of Parent/Guardian ______________________________

Total amount enclosed £____________

☐ **I enclose a cheque/postal order payable to Egmont Books Limited**

☐ **Please charge my MasterCard/Visa/Amex/Switch or Delta account** (delete as appropriate)

Card Number

Expiry date __/__ **Signature** ______________________________

Please allow 28 days for delivery. Offer is only available while stocks last. We reserve the right to change the terms of this offer at any time and we offer a 14 day money back guarantee. This does not affect your statutory rights. Data Protection Act: If you do not wish to receive other similar offers from us or companies we recommend, please tick this box ☐. Offers apply to UK only.

MR.MEN LITTLE MISS

CUT ALONG DOTTED LINE AND RETURN THIS WHOLE PAGE